THE FIDDLER OF HIGH LONESOME

THE FIDDLER

OF HIGH LONESOME

Written and Illustrated by **Brinton Turkle**

The Viking Press   New York

1524571

for Haynes

onder mountain is called High Lonesome. Nowadays, nobody lives up there—nobody but the critters. Not the big critters, just the little bitty ones like squirrels and rabbits and maybe a skunk or two. There's a old cabin without a roof on it and a dry well—all that's left of the last folks that lived up there. Name of Fogle.

The young one was Sud. He was six foot tall and he was the littlest. Next come Deet. He could whip Sud. Then there was Hunk. He was the oldest and he could whip both his brothers. Their pappy was Old Man Fogle. He was bigger than any of them and could whip them all. They done whatever he said.

Old Man Fogle allowed as how he once shot a deer and a bobcat and a gopher snake with just one bullet. The Fogles was all great hunters. And they made powerful corn whiskey. Somewhere up on High Lonesome was a still where they brewed it, hid away from the law. No one but the Fogles ever seen it.

One day a puny little fellow toting a couple of bundles come into the valley and started to climb High Lonesome. He got about halfway up when he got his hat shot off him. That was the way the Fogles said howdy to strangers.

"Don't shoot!" he called out. "I ain't the law. I'm yore kin." Well, even a one-eyed catbird could see he wasn't the law; but he sure didn't look like kin to the Fogles neither. "My mammy were a Fogle from Chickasaw Creek. My pappy were name of Bochamp. I is Lysander Bochamp."

Old Man Fogle come out from behind a rock. He cocked his rifle slow. "What do you want?" he said.

"My mammy taken sick and died last week," said the little fellow. "I reckoned I could bide with you for a spell. I'll work for my keep and I don't eat much."

"Where's yore pa?"

"He died too. A long time ago. No one left but me. Yore all the kinfolk I got."

Hunk and Deet and Sud come out from behind some bushes.

Old Man Fogle studied the little fellow like he was a fly he didn't know whether to swat or let go. By-and-by he spit and he said, "You know how to make corn whiskey?"

"No sir, I don't."

Old Man Fogle spit again and he said, "Kin you hunt?"

"No sir, I don't much favor shootin'."

Old Man Fogle took his time and then he said, "Well, yore goin' to see plenty of shootin' around here if you don't git and git fast. You ain't no kin of ourn."

"Yes I is! My mammy were a Fogle. Please let me bide with you. I'm lonesome all by myself."

"Boys," the old man said to his sons, "let's see if he kin dance a jig." The young Fogles raised their rifles and fired.

Bullets peppered the yellow dust around the little fellow's feet. He backtracked so fast, he stumbled and fell down. One of his bundles come undone. In it was a fiddle. He grabbed it quick. "Don't shoot!" he yelled. "I'm goin'!"

Now if there's one thing the folks around here has always liked, it's fiddle music; and there hadn't been a fiddler at Jellicoe's Mill in the hollow for a coon's age.

"Hold on there!" roared the old man. "What you doin' with that fiddle?"

"It were my pappy's."

"Kin you play it?"

"Tolerable."

"Let's hear you."

The little fellow didn't have to be spoke to twice. He done what he was told. He <u>tucked</u> the fiddle under his chin and begun to play. It wasn't loud, but it was sweet.

"Play somethin' pert and lively," Hunk said.

The fiddler struck up a reel. The boys and the old man begun tapping their toes and slapping their legs and pretty soon they was stomping and capering about like a herd of billy goats. The fiddler didn't quit till they was all tuckered out.

Old Man Fogle set down on a rock and fanned hisself with his hat. "Bochamp," he said, "kin you keep crows out of a corn patch?"

"I reckon so," said the fiddler.

"Then you kin bide with us fer a spell."

"I'm mighty obliged."

The old man stood up. "You'll earn yore keep, Bo-champ," he said.

"Name of Lysander," the little fellow said, quiet-like.

"That ain't no kind of a name," said the old man. "We callin' you Bochamp."

And that's how the fiddler come to bide on High Lonesome with the Fogles, because they was kin and he was scared of being alone.

But it wasn't a happy home for the little fellow. There was so much drinking and shooting and fighting going on amongst the Fogles, many a time he went by hisself up to the highest rock on High Lonesome and played his fiddle to the pine trees and the clouds. Sometimes, just before sundown, the wind would carry his music to the valley below. Folks claimed it made them remember times that was better and loved ones that was gone. Even the little bitty children would stop their playing and just listen.

When he wouldn't take a gun to the corn-patch, the Fogles said Lysander Bochamp was plumb crazy. The only way to keep crows from stealing corn, they said, was to shoot them.

"I throws stones at them," he said. "They gets the idea and I guarantee you won't lose much corn." And that was so, although he never once hit a crow and he had to keep right busy.

"Sure as shootin'," said the Fogles, "he ain't one of us!"

They got mighty riled when he wouldn't help them skin all the dead critters they brung home.

"What you want to do all that killin' for?" the little fellow said. "Them critters never harmed you."

"They's varmints!" said the Fogles. "Ever'body kills varmints! Git a knife, Bochamp, and lend a hand."

"They's critters. You killed 'em; you skin 'em. I won't have no truck with it," he said. And he went off to the woodpile to chop kindling.

The Fogles like to have skinned him. "Sure as shootin'," they grumbled, "he ain't one of us."

They'd have sent him away excepting for Saturday nights. Then the Fogles would carry him with them down to Jellicoe's Mill in the hollow to play for the dancing. Folks come from all over as soon as they heard about the new fiddler.

Aunt Sally Larkin sashayed around like she was
fifty year younger. "I ain't heerd playin' like that since
I were a girl," she told Old Man Fogle. "It's better for
my rheumatism than stump water."

"His mammy were a Fogle," the old man said.

"Well, I declare!"

Old Man Fogle strutted around as proud as a turkey
cock. "He's one of us," he said. "Sure as shootin'!"

One Saturday night the young Fogles was getting theirselves all slickered up to go dancing and they was wrangling as usual. This time it was over who had a turn at the mirror. As usual, Lysander Bochamp was trying to keep out of the way.

Like a cyclone, Old Man Fogle busted into the cabin. "Hush up!" he roared. "You boys want to bring the law up here?"

"Law? Where's the law?" Right away the young Fogles was reaching for their guns.

"They're down in the valley. Zed Harper's dead. They wrecked his still. I'm goin' over to our still and stand guard."

"We goin' with you," the boys said.

"You won't do no such a thing!" The old man smashed his fist down on the table. "Where's the sense you boys was born with? You all is goin' down to Jellicoe's Mill with Bochamp here the same as any other Saturday night. Anybody see the four of us in the hills tonight, they'd know somethin' was up. I kin handle this myself." He grabbed his gun and stomped out of the cabin.

If there ever was a chance for shooting, the young
Fogles hated to be left out of it. They fussed and grumbled all the way down to the mill. By the time they got
there, a full moon come up as big and bright as a new
skillet. It was a warm September night and just about
everybody turned out—especially the young ones who
was sparking.

In the middle of a do-si-do, Lysander Bochamp noticed that his kinfolk was missing. He stopped his fiddle playing and run outside just in time to see the Fogles going over the top of a hill. "Wait for me!" he shouted, and run after them.

"Go on back to your fiddlin'," said Deet.

"Don't leave me here. Carry me with you."

"Why, Bochamp?" said Sud. "You scared to go home alone?"

"No," said the little fellow; but he was lying. "Yore pappy said you wasn't to go to the still tonight."

Hunk grabbed him by his shirt. "Hush yore mouth, Bochamp," he said. "This ain't none of yore business. Now you go on back to the mill. The folks is lookin' fer you. Don't you fret. We be back in time to carry you home."

But the Fogles never come back. Lysander Bochamp played his fiddle until everybody went home and the mill was locked up. He stood outside in the moonlight waiting and waiting and getting lonesomer and lonesomer. He heard a couple of hooty owls and far away a hound dog howled and he remembered the stories folks told about spirits in the valley. He looked at the moon, and the moon looked at him. Then, he figured if he was to get back to High Lonesome before the moon set, he'd better make tracks because the Fogles wasn't coming. So he tucked his fiddle under his arm and started out.

The old Murdock place was still standing then, although nobody would live there. Folks used to say that Leester Murdock come back from the dead and sharpened his ax in the barn at the full of the moon. Lysander Bochamp had to pass that way. And he had to go

through the edge of Cottonmouth Swamp where the bullfrogs is so big they chase hound dogs and there's swampfire that lures you into the quicksand. He hurried on to get to the top of High Lonesome while he could still see, although a good bit of the way up the mountain was in shadows as black as the inside of your hat and he stumbled more than once.

Near the top he come to a little clearing where he stopped under a sassafras tree to catch his wind. Maybe the Fogles had just forgot. They was probably home right now snoring in their beds, or wrangling over something. Anybody could forget.

He was about to push on when a thought come to him that made him turn cold all over: What if the cabin was empty? What if the Fogles was never coming back? What if they had shot it out with the law somewhere on the mountainside? And what if they was laying there *dead*—all of them?

He heard something in the bushes and nearly jumped out of his skin. "Hunk?" he called. The Fogles might have remembered they left him down at the mill, and started out to meet him. "Deet? . . . Sud?"

There was no answer. But something was moving in the bushes.

He tried to call again. This time he couldn't make a sound. He couldn't move his feet neither, or he'd have been out of that clearing like a jack rabbit with its tail on fire.

But he could tuck his fiddle under his chin, and that's what he done. Somehow, he pulled the bow across the strings and music come out—it wasn't the best music he could play, but it was music. And the more he played, the better it sounded. It got livelier and livelier and pretty soon, he wasn't scared hardly at all.

Then something mighty peculiar happened: a little bear come out of the bushes and sure enough, it was dancing back and forth in time to his music! Then another bear come out, then a coon and a couple of foxes—they was all dancing! Two more bears come out—big granddaddy bears. Then a panther. Bochamp never seen a live one before. It danced around in circles. And then a whole family of skunks come out and even the little bitty ones was waving their tails in time to the music, trying to keep up with their mammy and pappy. It was so comical, Lysander Bochamp could hardly keep from laughing out loud.

He walked right out into the moonlight and played his fiddle while more critters come out and sashayed all around him. None of them was bothering the others! They was all pleasuring theirselves just like the folks in the hollow—and some of them was a lot better dancers!

As soon as the moon set, the critters stopped dancing and went back into the trees. In the afterlight, Lysander Bochamp made his way back to the cabin. He wasn't scared no more.

The Fogles was just going to bed when he come in.

"So you made it, Bochamp," said Deet.

"Yes, I made it."

Sud yawned. "We come on home by ourselves," he said. "We figured you knowed the way."

"Yes, I knowed the way."

"Zed Harper ain't dead," Hunk said. "His still was struck by lightnin'. 'Twasn't the law at all."

"That's good."

Old Man Fogle pulled down his galluses and scratched hisself. "What's ailin' you, boy?" he said, squinting at the little fellow. "You actin' like you is tetched."

"I ain't tetched," said Lysander Bochamp. And then he told them what he just seen.

When he was done, the old man shook his head. "Bochamp," he said, "you been out in the moonlight too long. Varmints don't dance."

"When I plays the fiddle, they do," said the little fellow, speaking up as if he was as big as Old Man Fogle hisself.

The boys all started laughing fit to bust.

"I'll show you!" said the little fiddler. "Tomorrow night, if there's a moon, I'll take you to the clearin' and you'll see."

All the next day the Fogles tormented Lysander Bochamp and give him no peace.

"Bochamp fixin' to give our jaybirds music lessons," Hunk said. They all thought that was mighty comical.

"I don't want no harm comin' to the critters tonight," the little fiddler said.

Deet said, "Why Bochamp, we is superfine gentle-men. We wouldn't harm no one. I'll say: 'Pardon me, Miz' Bear, may I have the honor of the next quadrille?'" They thought that was even more comical.

"I ain't fixin' to take you lessen you leaves yore guns behind."

Sud said, "Why, Mister Bochamp, we wouldn't think of totin' our guns to yore sociable. We'll leave them right here."

And they did. That night when the moon come up, Hunk and Deet and Sud all went snicker-ing after the little fiddler to the clearing. Old Man Fogle, he wouldn't go. He said he wasn't going lollygagging around High Lonesome like a body gone silly.

When they got to the clearing, Lysander Bochamp told them to stay quiet in the shade of the sassafras tree. "If you makes any noise, you'll scare the critters away," he said. Then he stepped out into the moonlight and drawed his bow across the fiddle strings.

The music was soft and low and trailed off into the sky like chimbley smoke. "Come out," it said, as sweet as you please. "Come out. Come out. Come out."

This time the foxes was first. Then some more little critters—coons and possums keeping time to the music just like the night before. The fiddler sort of played them out into the clearing. He looked over at the sassafras tree, but the shadows was so black, he couldn't see no-

body. It was a good thing the Fogles was keeping quiet for once.

Then, the big bears come out—it looked like the same ones that was dancing the night before—and two more good-sized cubs. It was wonderful how the big critters could dance so graceful. The fiddler played faster and faster and the panther come out and danced around in circles.

Then the shots rang out. There was a terrible commotion. There was more and more shots and the critters was growling and squealing and moaning, trying to get back to the trees, but most of them didn't make it.

Lysander Bochamp jumped over a coon that was thrashing around on the ground and run to the sassafras tree. "Stop it!" he yelled. "Stop it!"

"Git out of the way!" Deet yelled back.

The fiddler yanked Deet's gun away from him. Deet knocked him down with one swipe of his big hand and grabbed his gun back just in time to shoot a bear that was coming right at them.

"What in tarnation's the matter with you, Bochamp?" Deet said. "You like to git us both killed!"

More than a dozen critters lay dead and dying in the clearing. The Fogles come out hooting and hollering.

Old Man Fogle come out too, dancing a jig. "Hallelujah!" he yelled. "Hallelujah! I sure am glad you boys come fer me. I never seed such a thing in all my born days!" He kicked over the panther. "That's Old Sluefoot. Danged if I didn't git him after all these years!"

The boys was already wrangling over who shot the biggest bear.

"Hush up!" the old man roared. "You boys kin have

a dozen bears apiece—maybe a hundred. You know what we goin' to do? Ever' month when the moon is full, we goin' to carry Bochamp with us and he'll play the fiddle and we'll kill all the varmints on High Lonesome."

"Whoo-ee!" said Sud. "Mebbe all the varmints in the county!"

"Why, sure—all the varmints in the state!" said the old man. He marched over to the fiddler and hauled him to his feet and slapped him on the back. "You boys ought to be mighty proud of yore kin. Bochamp here is turnin' into some account after all."

Lysander Bochamp looked around the clearing. "Some-body give me a gun," he said.

"What you want a gun fer?" said Hunk.

"They's a little critter here is bad hurt. I wants to put it out'n its misery."

"Here," said Hunk.

The fiddler shot the coon that was jumping around on the ground making little noises and it was quiet. It didn't jump around no more. He handed the gun back to Hunk and picked up his fiddle. "I ain't no kin of yourn," he said, and walked off into the trees.

That was the last the Fogles ever seen of Lysander Bochamp. Nobody ever knowed for sure what become of him.

The Fogles didn't last long after that. The old man shot hisself while he was cleaning a gun. The boys killed off all the big critters on High Lonesome. Then the well run dry and they just went away. "Good riddance," most of the folks in the valley said. But they sure missed the little fiddler.

Sometimes when the moon is full you can hear strange sounds in the hills if you listen careful. Wild and sweet sounds. "It's only the wind," some folks say. But there's others that say, "Hark! Its the fiddler of High Lonesome. He's playin' for his critters tonight."